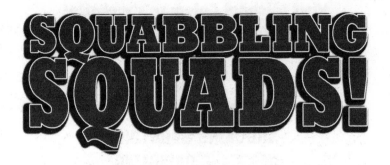

SQUABBLING SQUADS!

AND OTHER STORIES:

HANDBALL HORROR

MIDFIELD MADNESS

MICHAEL COLEMAN

ILLUSTRATED BY NICK ABADZIS

ORCHARD BOOKS

Visit Michael Coleman's website!
www.michael-coleman.com

Look out for the other Angels FC books:

SHOCKING SHOOTING
DAZZLING DRIBBLING
TOUCHLINE TERROR
AWESOME ATTACKING

ORCHARD BOOKS
338 Euston Road, London NW1 3BH
Orchard Books Australia
Level 17/205 Kent St, Sydney, NSW 2000

First published in Great Britain as individual volumes
First published in Great Britain in this bind-up format 2004
This edition published 2008
Midfield Madness
Text © Michael Coleman 1998, inside illustrations © Nick Abadzis 1998
Handball Horror
Text © Michael Coleman 1997, inside illustrations © Nick Abadzis 1997
Squabbling Squads, publishing for the first time as part of this bind-up
Text © Michael Coleman 2004, inside illustrations © Nick Abadzis 2004

ISBN 978 1 40830 013 8

1 3 5 7 9 10 8 6 4 2
Printed in Great Britain by
CPI Cox & Wyman, Reading, RG1 8EX

Orchard Books is a division of Hachette Children's Books
an Hachette Livre UK company.
www.hachettelivre.co.uk

A HILARIOUS HAT TRICK OF STORIES!

ANGELS FC!

Goalkeeper

Left Full Back

Right Full Back

Midfield (Centre)

Centre Back

Striker

Co[...]

Kirsten Browne

Barry 'Bazza' Watts

Tarlock Bhasin

Lennie Gould (Captain)

Daisy Higgins

Colin 'Co[...] Flower[...]

Midfield
(Centre)

Striker

Substitute

Centre
Back

Midfield
(Left)

Substitute

Midfield
(Right)

Mick
Ryall

Lulu Squibb

Jeremy
Emery

Rhoda
O'Neill

Lionel
Murgatroyd

Trev the
Rev

Jonjo
Rix

Ricky
King

SQUABBLING SQUADS

CONTENTS

1

Welcome!

It was a Friday evening, and the twelve members of St. Jude's Youth Club were holding their regular get-together. Or, rather, NOT-get-together!

"The trouble with *girls*," said the strong, powerful voice of Lennie Gould, "is that they're totally useless at things that matter – like *football*!"

"And the trouble with *boys*," retorted Daisy Higgins, in her only slightly less powerful voice, "is that they've all got heads like footballs – *filled with air*!"

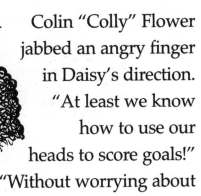

Colin "Colly" Flower jabbed an angry finger in Daisy's direction. "At least we know how to use our heads to score goals!"

"Without worrying about messing our hair up!" sneered Jonjo Rix.

From the other end of the room Rhoda O'Neill swung round and pointed at Jonjo. "Only because you haven't got any hair worth messing up!"

Mick Ryall peered through his glasses at Jonjo's shaven head. "She's right y'know."

"She is not right!" yelled burly Barry Watts. "Girls are never right! Ain't that right, Lionel?"

Lionel Murgatroyd frowned uncertainly. "Er…well…it is possible…technically…on the odd occasion…" A sharp jab in the ribs from Barry made his mind up for him. "No, Bazza!" he yelped. "Girls are never right!"

Lulu Squibb took an angry step forward, pulling Kirsten Browne with her. "You big bananas! You think you're best at everything. But none of you is a better goalie than Kirsten!"

"Only because she can catch the ball in her mouth!" laughed Jeremy Emery.

"And still carry on talking!" giggled Tarlock Bhasin.

This was too much. Kirsten marched angrily towards the centre of the room. "Are you suggesting that we girls talk too much?"

Lennie, tall and powerful like his voice, stomped forward to meet her. "No, we're not suggesting that."

"Oh…"

"We're *saying* it!" yelled Lennie. "Because it's a *fact*!"

The other boys stalked forward to join their leader. On the opposite side, Daisy, Lulu and Rhoda hurried to stand shoulder-to-shoulder with Kirsten. Within moments the air was filled with insults.

If they'd been asked, none of them would have been able to explain exactly why they argued so much. It was simply the way it had always been. Boys against girls. Girls against boys. Football, darts, table tennis – they'd argue over anything. Sometimes they'd even argue over which side was better at arguing!

"Right!" Lennie Gould finally yelled above the noise. "There's only one way to settle this! A contest!"

Daisy hesitated. "Er…shouldn't we wait for the new vicar to turn up?"

St Jude's Youth Club was linked to St Jude's Church. The church's vicar had just retired and they'd all been told that the new one – a Reverend T. Rowe – was due to arrive that very day. When he hadn't been around at their usual starting time they'd assumed he wasn't coming and just opened up themselves.

"Shouldn't we wait for the new vic-ah?" taunted Bazza, making fun of Daisy. "Excuses!" Jeremy joined in. "Daisy doesn't dare!" he laughed. They were off again.

"Oh yes, she does!" shouted Kirsten.

"Oh, yeah?" bawled Jonjo.

"Yeah!" screamed Daisy.

Her temper was well and truly up now. But even at its peak it was a molehill compared to Lulu Squibb's.

"Come on, then!" challenged Lulu. "I've got a tennis ball. We'll see who's got the most football skill – right here and now!"

15

"Right here?" echoed Colly, looking around.

Lulu didn't answer. She was pushing chairs against the wall. Only after she, Daisy, Rhoda and Kirsten had carried the table-tennis table into the middle of the room did she explain what she was thinking.

"Table-tennis football," she said.

Lennie was scratching his head. "What?"

"Two-a-side," replied Lulu. "But instead of table-tennis bats we have to use our heads and feet."

Daisy laughed. It was her turn to sneer nastily. "A true test of skill, boys. That's if you're brave enough…"

Lennie jumped forward immediately, Jonjo beside him. "You're on! Me and Jonjo…"

"Against me and Daisy!" yelled Lulu, brandishing her tennis ball. "And may the best team win!"

"Us!" yelled everybody else as they leapt on to chairs to watch.

Lulu began the game by lobbing the tennis ball over the net to bounce on the boys' side of the table. Lennie ducked forward in a flash, heading the ball back over the net to land on the girls' side. Daisy played it craftily. Waiting until the ball had cleared the end of the table, she swung her right foot and volleyed it back hard and low to Jonjo's side.

17

"Aaah!" he shouted, stretching frantically for the ball. With a desperate flick of his foot, he just managed to lob the ball high into the air and over the net.

Now it was Lulu's turn to panic. The fact that Jonjo hadn't been able to get much power behind his return was going to count in the boys' favour. Instead of coming straight back to her it was going to dribble over the net and land just on their side of the table. Lulu knew they'd lose the point! Unless…

Lulu did the only thing she could think of. Leaping onto the table, she lunged for the ball, toe-ending it like a rocket. The effect was dramatic.

"Aaagh!" screeched Lennie Gould as it hit him in the eye. "Waaahh" wailed Lulu as, unable to stop, she slithered further along the table, tripped over its thin green net, and flew into the air! Her only thought, then, was to find a soft landing place.

She found one. Jonjo. Throwing out her arms, Lulu grabbed him round the neck at the same moment as she wrapped her legs around his waist. Jonjo felt like he'd been hit by a cannonball. Staggering backwards, he fell in a painful heap with Lulu crashing down on top of him.

19

He wasn't the only one in agony. As she'd seen Lulu begin sailing through the air, Daisy had darted forward to try and save her. She hadn't got far. Lulu's weight had caused the table-tennis table to collapse. Daisy had tripped over one of its legs and ploughed headlong into the nearest of the spectators: Lionel Murgatroyd. Like the others, Lionel had been standing on a chair at the side of the room. Hit by the galloping Daisy, he toppled backwards – straight into Jeremy, standing on a chair at his side. Jeremy went over, thumped into Rhoda…so that, like falling dominos, every one of the spectators was soon on the floor with

chairs tumbling down around their heads.

All in all, then, it was an embarrassing moment for the door to open and someone to walk in. But open it did, with the newcomer announcing his arrival even before he'd stepped into the room.

"Hello, everyone! I'm the new vicar. Trevor Rowe's my name. Call me…Trev."

With Lennie holding his eye, Lulu and Jonjo groaning on the floor and everybody else looking as if they were fighting with a chair, only Daisy was able to summon up a reply.

"Hello, er – Trev. Welcome to the, er…Youth Club. Ha-ha."

2

Challenge Match

Lennie glared at Daisy. "You've asked for this and now you're gonna get it!"

Daisy glared straight back. "The only thing we're gonna get," she snarled, "is plenty of goals!"

A shrill peep of a whistle interrupted this unfriendly discussion. In the centre of a makeshift pitch marked out with plastic cones, stood Trev, their new vicar.

"Ready to start, then?" he shouted.

The game had been his idea. After

getting them all to put the Youth Club room back to normal following the pandemonium of Lulu's table tennis football disaster, Trev the Rev (as they were already calling him behind his back) had sat them all down and listened without a word to the boys' moans about the girls and the girls' moans about the boys.

"Right," he'd said at the end. "Football gear, Sunday. A boys versus girls football match. Meet me in the park straight after Morning Service."

So they'd all turned up to find that while they'd gone home to get changed, he'd beaten them to it by coming straight from the church to the park.

Lennie shook his head. "What does he look like?"

"A plonker," said Daisy.

"Got it in one," agreed Lennie.

The vicar was still clad in his long black clerical frock, with the whistle dangling round his neck. From beneath the hem of his frock peeped the toes of a pair of football boots.

Sniggering behind their hands at this curious sight, the twelve players gathered in the centre of the pitch.

"As there are only four girls, I suggest a four-a-side game. The boys can sort themselves into two teams and swap over when they feel like it. Right?"

Bazza Watts sniffed. "No good. We all wanna smash 'em. All the time!"

Surprisingly, Rhoda agreed with him – but for a different reason. "That way they'll have a fresh team coming on and we won't. It won't be a fair match."

"But eight against four isn't fair either, is it?" said Trev.

"It would be if you made four of them play on their knees," argued Lulu. "That way it'd be an eight-legs-a-side!"

Trev rubbed his chin thoughtfully. "I think I've got a better idea," he said with a smile. "How about if I play on the girl's side?"

Lennie hooted. "Why not. I mean, you are wearing a frock!"

"You agree, then?" said Trev.

The boys all nodded enthusiastically. It was the girls who looked doubtful.

"Have you ever played football before?" asked Lulu.

25

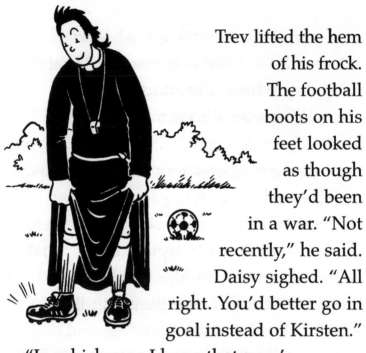

Trev lifted the hem of his frock. The football boots on his feet looked as though they'd been in a war. "Not recently," he said. Daisy sighed. "All right. You'd better go in goal instead of Kirsten."

"In which case I hope that gear's washable, Trev," said Colly. "'Cos you're going to get real muddy diving about."

"No, he isn't," retorted Lulu, "'cos the ball's going to be down your end all the time!"

"Oh, yeah?" shouted Lennie.

"Yeah!" shouted Daisy. "C'mon, let's get this fight started!"

26

⚽   ⚽   ⚽

In spite of being fewer in number, the girls
went straight onto the attack. A quick
one-two between Rhoda and Lulu put
Rhoda through on goal. Lionel Murgatroyd,
who'd been put between the posts because
he really wasn't terribly good anywhere
else, rushed out. Luck was on his side.
Swinging wildly with his left foot, he made
clean contact with the ball to thump it off
Rhoda's toes and send it sailing upfield to
where Colly Flower was lurking.

Without hesitating, Colly trapped the ball.
In one quick move he pushed it past Daisy
and smashed it goalwards. It was a
winner all the way.

"Yeah!" he began to crow, "one-nil to the boyyyy…"

The words died on his lips as he saw something which made his eyes pop. Not only had Trev the Rev saved his shot – he hadn't bothered to use his hands! Instead he'd trapped the ball on his chest…

let it fall to his thigh, flicked it quickly across to his other foot, then volleyed it back to Rhoda at the other end of the pitch! All she had to do was slide it past Lionel for the opening goal.

"Nearly right, Colly!" yelled Daisy. "It is one-nil...but to the girls!"

"Beginner's luck," muttered Jonjo, looking sideways at Trev as he put the ball down for the boys to kick off again.

Lennie was beside him, scowling. "He won't do that to one of your shots, Jonjo. Go on, sort him out."

Lennie kicked-off, touching the ball to Jonjo. Immediately, the powerful striker raced for the goal. Shrugging off a tackle by Kirsten, he pushed the ball forward. Both Lulu and Daisy slid in – but they were too late. Darting between them, Jonjo had the ball at his feet and only Trev to beat.

Jonjo got ready to let fly, only to change his mind. Blasting the ball past the vicar would be too easy. He was going to show him how football should be played and dribble round him!

Trev, frock flapping, was coming out from his goal. Oozing with confidence, Jonjo tapped the ball quickly to one side of him then ran round the other side to collect it. Too easy!

Except…where was the ball?

Everybody else knew, because they'd seen clearly what had happened. As the ball had gone to his side, Trev had put his foot on it like a flash. Even now he was dribbling forward himself.

"Leave him to me, boys!" thundered Lennie.

Vicar or no vicar, he was going to be launched into orbit. Lennie flew in – only to find himself tackling thin air. In a blur of movement Trev had dragged the ball back with the sole of his foot, flicked it up, then back-heeled it over Lennie's head as he'd charged at him like a runaway bulldozer. Then, before the other boys could move, the vicar had threaded an inch-perfect pass through for Rhoda to score again.

Lennie looked at Jonjo. Jonjo looked at Colly. Colly looked at Lennie. All three of them looked at the others. Not one of them said a word. They didn't have to. They were all thinking the same thing – that they'd made a big, big mistake!

3

Take notice

"Twenty-eight goals to nil!" crowed Daisy at the next Youth Club meeting. "And you were lucky to get nil!"

Lennie, with the rest of the boys sulking behind him, simply glowered and said nothing. The girls, though, had plenty to say.

"Trev's fantastic, isn't he?" chirped Kirsten.

"My favourite player," sighed Rhoda theatrically.

"Even though he must have been a boy once," laughed Lulu.

Daisy summed things up. "We girls have had a vote and decided that we like Trev the Rev!" She winked at Lennie. "What about you lot?"

Lennie finally broke his silence. "We like him even less than we like you lot – and that's saying something!"

"Oh dear," came a voice from the doorway. "I didn't expect you boys to be bad losers, Lennie." It was Trev, carrying a sheet of paper and a box of drawing pins.

"We're not bad losers," retorted Tarlock.

"Twenty-eight nil? Sounds like you're pretty bad losers to me!" hooted Daisy.

Bazza raised his voice. "Lennie means it wasn't a fair game. They had you," he said, pointing a finger at Trev. "How did you get to be such a brilliant player?"

"I had a good coach," smiled Trev.

"It takes more than that," replied Lennie, angry but admiring at the same time. "You must have been good enough to turn professional. Why didn't you?"

Trev's smile grew broader. "Because I wanted to become a vicar more. Anyway, aren't you forgetting something? I didn't score a single goal. All I ever did was pass to the girls. They had to finish things off."

"Your passes were so good, they couldn't miss!" scoffed Jeremy. "An ostrich with bad feet could have scored those goals."

Rhoda clenched both her fists. "Oh, yeah? Then how about a re-match?"

"So you're giving up football altogether, are you boys?" asked Trev.

As he was speaking, he moved across to the new notice board that had appeared on the wall since the previous Club night. In the middle of the green surface he pinned the sheet of paper he'd brought in with him.

"Pity," he said. "Because I thought you might find this interesting. Ah, well. Have a look anyway. Maybe you'll change your minds."

Reluctantly, Lennie and the others gathered round. Behind them the girls couldn't resist having a peep as well.

WANTED

Enthusiastic boys to join a NEW football team.
First training session this Saturday 11am, in the park.
Trevor Rowe (coach)

"Boys?!" screeched Daisy. "What about us girls?"

"Sorry, Daisy," said Trev. "You're not needed on Saturday."

It was the boys' turn to gloat and the girls' turn to glower. "A new team!" yelled Mick after Trev had left the room.

"With an all-star player as our coach!" whooped Colly.

Lennie couldn't resist it. "Us boys have changed our minds, Daisy. We like him after all. How about you lot?"

Daisy didn't need to ask the other girls. "We've changed our minds as well. Now we like him even less than we like you lot!"

4

Selection Setbacks

The boys were raring to go. Trev had come along to the training session armed with full playing kits for them all: white shirts, blue shorts and blue stockings. The only things missing were the badges on the shirts.

"There's a reason for that," explained Trev. "A badge should reflect the team's name and I haven't decided what you should be called yet."

"How about St Jude's Youth Club Rebels?" suggested Lennie brightly.

Trev frowned. "Hmm. Doesn't sound quite what I'm looking for, Lennie. And it would be a bit of a mouthful for our supporters."

"Good point," laughed Jonjo. "By the time my mum had finished shouting, 'Come on you St Jude's Youth Club Rebels!' the game would be over!"

Lionel put his hand up uncertainly. "So…er…we really are going to be a real team, then? And play real matches? Against other real teams?" Much as Lionel loved playing football at every opportunity, he knew he wasn't that good at the game – in or out of goal. The thought of a real match was making his stomach feel like an over-pumped ball.

So it didn't help when Trev said:

"That's right, Lionel! Starting next week. I've arranged a friendly game for the team already!"

"Wow!" shouted Lennie. "Five-a-side match, is it?"

"I'll tell you all about it later," smiled Trev. "After we've finished training. Come on, let's get cracking!"

Daisy, Rhoda, Lulu and Kirsten sat back and gave each other satisfied nods. While the boys were practising their dribbling, tackling and shooting – plus, in poor Lionel's case, their goalkeeping – they were practising something else. Seated round the table in Daisy's front room, they were practising their skills at protest-letter writing…

Dear Trev,

We really, really, really object to you leaving {US} out of your football team. This is why:

KIRSTEN is the BEST goalkeeper around. — MUCH better than Lionel. → He'd have trouble stopping a beach ball kicked by a baby!

DAISY is a stronger tackler than Tarlock or Bazza and much stronger than Jeremy. He's so feeble a strong wind could knock him over.

LULU has got more energy than Mick and Lennie put together (and even if you put them together you still wouldn't have a decent player!)

RHODA has a straighter → shot than either Colly or Jonjo. They'd be luckier as fish than footballers - because they never find the net! If you've got any sense you'll pick {US} for your first match.

Signed: Daisy Higgins   Kirsten Browne   Lulu Grubb   Rhoda O'Neill

"Perfect," said Kirsten.

"Now what?" said Lulu and Rhoda together.

Daisy folded the letter and tucked it in the pocket of her jeans. "Now we deliver it!" she said firmly.

⚽   ⚽   ⚽

Back on the training pitch, things weren't going as well as the boys had hoped. Trev's coaching had been great, with stacks of good ideas. The trouble had been putting them into practice.

Shooting from a distance, for example. Jonjo and Colly had done really well close to goal, but they hadn't been so hot when Trev had rolled passes for them to hit from the edge of the penalty area. Too many of Colly's shots had dribbled along the ground.

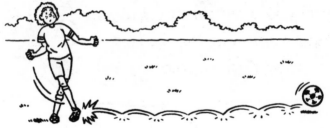

As for Jonjo, many of his thunderbolts had gone so high the local pigeons had been in greater danger than the goal!

Then there'd been tackling. Jeremy's long legs were perfect for sliding tackles. But when Jonjo had tackled him back all Jeremy had done was stop and bawl, "Trev! He touched me!"

In midfield, Mick wasn't as fit as he could be. His dribbling was fantastic, but after every mazy run he'd had to sit down to recover.

43

The biggest problem of all, though, had been in goal. Lionel was truly hopeless. He'd let shots go through his legs. He'd let the ball slip out of his hands. He'd thrown it out to the wrong players. And on one awful occasion he'd managed all four when, just as he was going to throw the ball out, he changed his mind, lost his grip – and knocked the ball through his own legs into the net!

Throughout all this, Trev had been quietly making notes. Now, with a sharp blast on his whistle, he gathered them round.

"Well done," he said. He glanced at his clipboard. "All we need to do now is decide a couple of things about your first match."

"Like who's going to be the substitutes, eh Trev?" said Lennie. "I mean, it's a five-a-side match and there's eight of us."

Lionel put his hand up at once. "Please can I be a sub? I'm not ready for a real game yet. I'd be too nervous. I wouldn't be at my best."

"If that's what you want, Lionel," said Trev. "It gives us a problem, though. We need another goalkeeper. Any suggestions?"

"Er...well..." murmured Lionel, avoiding the other boys' eyes, "I wouldn't tell her myself, but...well...Kirsten's a good goalie." He thought of adding "for a girl", but didn't.

Trev rubbed his chin thoughtfully. "I can ask her if she'd be interested in playing, I suppose. Anything else?"

Mick gave an embarrassed cough. "We…er…we could do with a strong tackler in defence as well. Someone sort of…well…Daisy-ish, maybe?"

"And we need something extra in midfield!" retaliated an offended Jeremy with a glare at Mick. "Someone who can run around a lot without having to stop for oxygen – someone like, er…oh, like Lulu!"

Colly and Jonjo looked at each other. "Someone with a good, long shot would help us," said Jonjo finally.

"Rhoda hits a lot of lucky ones," added Colly.

"Hang on, hang on!" yelled Bazza. "If all four of them play that only leaves room in the team for one of us!"

"Why?" asked Trev.

"Because you said you'd fixed up a five-a-side game," said Tarlock.

"No, I didn't. You asked if it was five-a-side. I said I'd tell you after training. Now I am. It's an eleven-a-side match."

"Eleven!" cried Lennie. "Then…there'll be enough places for all of us!"

"With me as substitute!" chirped Lionel.

Trev grinned and turned his clipboard their way. It didn't have a single note on it, just a team line-up.

"But – if you wanted girls in the team all along, why didn't you say so?" cried Lennie.

"Would you lot have been happy with the idea?" asked Trev.

Around him, heads shook slowly.

"That's what I thought. You had to discover for yourselves that the team would be better with them. All of you – boys and girls – are good players in your different ways."

He got to his feet. "As I'm sure the girls will be delighted to hear!"

Trev had not long returned to his small house next to St Jude's Church when a determined Daisy rang at the doorbell. Stationed behind her, Kirsten and Rhoda looked like soldiers preparing to go into battle. As for Lulu, she seemed to be impersonating a volcano that was about to erupt.

"Ah!" said Trev. "Just the people I wanted to see. The boys all agree – they want the four of you in the team for our first game next week."

Daisy felt as if a rocket shot had hit her right in the stomach. "They...do?"

"Definitely," said Trev. Quickly he fetched his clipboard to show them the team. Lulu erupted with laughter. Rhoda roared. Kirsten cackled. Daisy was delighted. They all were.

"Brilliant!" shouted Daisy. "We'll play!"

"Excellent," said Trev. "So – what did you come to see me about? Delivering a letter?"

Panic-stricken, Daisy looked at the letter she was holding. Quickly, she jammed it down the inside of the sports bag at her feet. "Letter? Ha-ha! That's not a letter, Trev! It's…er…my mum's shopping list! That's what it is. We were off to the park for a kick-about and going to the shops afterwards and we thought, 'I wonder if Trev wants any shopping?' Didn't we girls?"

She turned to see Kirsten, Lulu and Rhoda nodding their heads so hard it was starting to hurt.

Trev smiled. "No thanks, girls. I've got everything I want – now. See you at the match!"

5

Teamwork

"Ready, everybody?"

The whole squad replied as one:
"Ready, Trev!"

Trev called them into the centre of the
changing room for his pre-match
instructions. "The team you're against
have played together for a while now, so
you'll need good teamwork to beat them.
They're called Cropley Colts."

"Have you decided what *we're* going to
be called, Trev?" asked Lennie.

"Not yet, Lennie. We'll have to be St Jude's for now. Maybe I'll have a good idea during the game. So, out you go!"

Daisy was the last to dash out. "And what do you have to remember, Daisy?" asked Trev.

Daisy gave her sports bag an excited kick. "Teamwork!" she yelled. "No squabbling in the squad!"

⚽   ⚽   ⚽

Full of enthusiasm, the new team kicked off. Cropley were well organised though, and for most of the first half there were few chances at either end. With Daisy and Jeremy combining well, and Kirsten in good form, the score was still at 0-0 when Lennie won the ball in midfield.

Up front, Colly and Jonjo were being closely marked. But, dashing forward with enough energy for two players, was Lulu. Lennie slid a perfect pass through to her.

As a Cropley defender ran to meet her, Jonjo
darted into the space he'd left. Lulu
quickly slid the ball to him, Jonjo
turned – and hammered the ball home!
They were 1-0 ahead!

"Great teamwork, everybody," shouted
Trev. "Keep it going. Only a couple of
minutes to half-time!"

Beside him, Lionel was bouncing up and
down eagerly, wanting to play a part in
some way. "Anything I can do, Trev?"

Trev fished in his pocket and handed him
a key. "Fetch the half-time drinks please,
Lionel. I've left them in the changing room."

Lionel raced off. Unlocking the changing-room door, he saw the crate of drinks bottles at once. He snatched them up – and stopped as he almost trod on what looked like a letter. A letter, unknown to him, that had flown from the sports bag Daisy had so enthusiastically kicked. It didn't take Lionel long to read…

Neither did Daisy's letter take the other boys long to read as they passed it stealthily from one to the other during the half-time break.

"Feeble, am I?" snarled Jeremy under his breath.

"Would be better fish than footballers?" hissed Jonjo and Colly to each other.

"Mick and me *put together* wouldn't make a decent player?" muttered Lennie when the letter came to him. He screwed it into a ball and hurled it furiously into the drinks-bottle crate sitting beside the touchline.

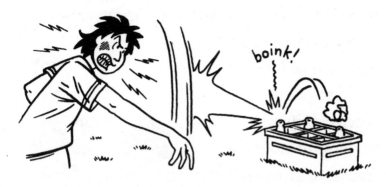

The referee's whistle shrieked, calling them for the start of the second half. Trev cupped his hands to his mouth. "Teamwork, everybody!" he yelled.

But Lennie had a message of his own. "Forget teamwork, lads," he muttered in every boy's ear. "We're doing no work. We're on strike!"

The second half began slowly. The Cropley team, surprised at how well their opponents had played in the first half, were nervous about taking too many chances. But suddenly that all changed. Latching on to a hopeful pass, Cropley's striker ran towards the defensive duo of Daisy and Jeremy.

"Tackle him, Jeremy!" yelled Daisy.

Jeremy stood his ground, arms folded. "What, feeble little me? Not likely. You're the strong one. Tackle him yourself!"

"You tell her, Jez!" shouted Tarlock and Bazza.

"But…you're faster than me!" wailed Daisy, trying to catch up with Cropley's striker. She got nowhere near him.

Unchallenged, he banged the ball past Kirsten to make the score 1-1.

"Wh-what's the matter?" asked Daisy as they lined up again.

"We found your little letter, that's what," snapped Lennie. "So, as of now, this is a boys-only team. As far as we're concerned, you girls are invisible. Hear that, boys?"

"But—"

Lennie wasn't in the mood to listen. Stomping forward to take the kick-off, he slid the ball to Jonjo. Charging straight for goal, Jonjo quickly found two Cropley defenders barring his way. Suddenly he heard a shout from his left. Rhoda was in the clear.

"Pass!" she screamed.

"No!" yelled Jonjo back. "I'm not passing to a girl!"

Instead he tried to thread the ball through to Colly, only for a Cropley defender to intercept the pass easily and hammer the ball forward to his winger. Bazza Watts had seen the trouble coming, though. Racing across, he took the ball off the winger's toe.

"Pass back!" yelled Kirsten, coming out of her goal.

"Jump in the lake, girlie-goalie!" shouted Bazza angrily. But he had to do something. He was facing the wrong way and the Cropley winger was breathing down his neck.

Suddenly he saw Lionel, standing behind the goal to save stray shots going out into the road. He was a boy. He'd pass to him!

Leaning back, Bazza gave the ball a thump. Over Kirsten's head it sailed – but not over the crossbar as he'd intended. It dipped just beneath it instead. An own goal! They were 2-1 down!

"Useless boys!" ranted Kirsten as the Colts players began celebrating all around her. "Why ever did we agree to play with you!"

"Pathetic girls!" Bazza raged back. "Why ever did we *ask* you to play with us!"

In an instant the whole pitch was filled with insults. The shouting spread so quickly that none of them noticed Trev unfold the screwed-up ball of paper he'd seen Lennie throw away before the second half began. Nor did they see him smile to himself. No, they only noticed their coach when he interrupted the arguing to call Lennie over to the touchline.

There, he whispered something in his captain's ear. Lennie frowned. Trev whispered again. This time Lennie nodded, then ran cheerfully back.

"What did he say?" asked Mick.

"Tell you later," grinned Lennie.

The Cropley Colts were finally getting back into position after celebrating the goal. It gave Trev just enough time to signal Daisy over. She didn't hurry, expecting to be given a good telling-off. So it came as a complete shock when Trev said, "Lennie just said sorry. He agrees the girls are playing like Angels."

Daisy goggled. "He did? He does? Really."

"Really," said Trev.

61

"Well, in that case…" beamed Daisy. She charged back onto the pitch and straight up to Lennie. "We're sorry too. The boys are playing great as well." She swung round to call to Kirsten, Lulu and Rhoda: "Teamwork, girls!"

"Yeah?" frowned Lennie. Then…great!" It was his turn to bellow. "You heard what the lady said, lads – teamwork!"

The effect was instantaneous. No sooner had they kicked off than the ball was switched out to Mick. He launched himself into a mazy dribble. Reaching the by-line he heard Jonjo calling for a pass. But, sprinting towards the penalty area, Rhoda was yelling too – and she was completely unmarked. Ignoring Jonjo, Mick pulled the ball back for Rhoda to blast it high into the Cropley net. 2-2!

Cropley fought back, but good defending from Jeremy and Daisy kept them out. With just a couple of minutes to go the duo did the same again, quickly closing down the Cropley striker so that he hurried his shot and blasted it well wide of the goal.

"I'll get it, Kirsten!" yelled Lionel, dashing after the ball.

Lionel hurriedly kicked it back, enabling Kirsten to take a smart, short goal-kick to Tarlock. He played it to Jeremy, Jeremy switched it to Daisy and she slid it sideways to Bazza. The tactic worked. Tempted forward, some of the Cropley players were out of position when Bazza drove the ball through to Lennie. He hit a quick pass to Lulu and she spun it on to Mick. No mazy dribble this time. Mick played a clever forward pass to Jonjo – who looked up to see Rhoda running through unmarked yet again! Taking Jonjo's pass in her stride, she feinted to hammer a shot but, this time, as the Cropley goalie was fooled into diving one way, simply played a square pass to Colly. All he had to do was run the ball into the net to make the score 3-2!

"Yeah!" bawled Lennie. "An eleven-player move!"

"A twelve-player move, you mean," laughed Kirsten. "Lionel gave it to me!"

"Well done, boys and girls," said Trev as the players gathered round him at the end. "A win in your first game together."

"Thanks to the girls," said Mick. "They all played brilliantly."

"And thanks to the boys," said Lulu. "They were just as brilliant."

Daisy stepped forward. "But most of all, thanks to Lennie," she said. "If he hadn't apologised…"

"What!" yelped Lennie. "What are you on about? I didn't apologise!"

Daisy wagged a finger under his nose. "Yes, you did! Trev told me. 'Lennie just said sorry. He agrees the girls are playing like Angels.' They were his exact words."

"I did not say sorry!" yelled Lennie.

"You did," smiled Trev. "When I told you my idea for a team name you didn't hear it first time. You said 'sorry?' and I repeated it."

"But that wasn't saying sorry to Daisy!"

"I didn't tell her that. I just told her that you'd said sorry – which was true. And what team name did I suggest, Lennie?"

"Angels FC."

"A stroke of inspiration," said Trev. "And you agreed it was a good name."

Lionel had seen through the trick. "So what Trev said was true. You did agree the girls were playing like Angels. Because we all were. Including me!"

They were all laughing now, Lennie and Daisy loudest of all as they realised how cleverly Trev had tricked them. Grinning broadly, they shook hands.

"Rivalry over," said Lennie.

"Definitely," said Daisy. "From now on, it's boys and girls together."

"Seeing the good things about each other instead of the bad things!" shouted Lionel, surprising everybody with his passion. "And I'm not talking about my goalkeeping, either. The team plays better if we're friends instead of enemies."

"Well said, Lionel," said Trev. "And very appropriate – because I've just had another thought. A team slogan."

He told them what it was, then raised his hands like an orchestra's conductor. "Right? Let's hear it. All together, now…"

HANDBALL
HORROR

CONTENTS

1

Picky Ricky

Jonjo Rix gazed out of his bedroom window with interest. There wasn't often something happening outside that could drag him away from his favourite *Super Soccer* video game, but today was such a day. Next door, new neighbours were moving in.

What was more, one of them was a boy of about his own age. Tall and well-built, the boy looked as if he might be a good footballer – except for the fact that, in all the time he'd been watching the removal van being unloaded, Jonjo hadn't seen any sign of a football being carried in.

A baseball bat – yes.

A fielder's glove, as used in baseball – yes.

Shoulder pads, thigh pads, and an American football shirt – yes.

An oval ball, as used in American football – yes.

But a real, round football? No.

There was only one thing to do, decided Jonjo: go and take a look. Hopping downstairs, he went out onto the small square of grass they called a front garden.

"Hey, Mac!"

Jonjo looked round. The boy he'd seen from his window was shouting at somebody. Only when the boy called again did it occur to Jonjo that he was the one being shouted at.

"You talking to me?"

"Sure am." The boy approached the low hedge that divided the two front gardens. "What's your name?"

74

"Well it isn't Mac, for starters. It's John Joseph Rix. But everybody calls me Jonjo."

"OK. I'm Ricky," said the boy. "Ricky King. I'm from Dallas, in America. My dad's over here on a work assignment."

Jonjo decided to get to the important question quickly. "Dallas got a football team have they?"

Ricky King's eyes lit up. "Have Dallas got a football team? Man, the Dallas Cowboys are only the biggest and best football team in the whole U. S. of A!"

Dallas Cowboys? What a name! thought Jonjo. Why couldn't they call themselves something normal, like 'Dallas United'? He was just wondering whether Manchester United would have been his favourite team if they'd been called 'Manchester Cowboys'

instead, when a shout came from inside the neighbouring house.

"Ricky!" It sounded American, and angry.

"Uh-oh. Better be going. I think she's found it."

"Who? Found what?"

"My mom," said Ricky. "Say, is your place as pokey as ours?"

"Pokey?"

"Pokey. Y'know, small! I just tried a couple of swings with my baseball bat like I do in my room at home and knocked a hole in the door."

Another shout came from inside, louder this time. "Ricky!!"

"Coming, Mom!" yelled Ricky. He turned away, then stopped to fire a final question at Jonjo. "Say, where does everyone hang out round here?"

"Hang out?"

"Gee, I thought you guys invented English! I mean where's the action round here? What do kids do?"

Jonjo fell in. "Oh. There's a youth club. St Jude's. We go there Friday and Sunday evenings."

"Swell. Mind if I tag along next Friday?"

"No. That'd be, er...swell," said Jonjo.

But he wasn't so sure.

⚽   ⚽   ⚽

"This is it?"

Ricky King's eyebrows shot skywards as Jonjo confirmed that, yes, this was St Jude's Youth Club.

"Gee," said Ricky, blowing out his cheeks as he gazed round St Jude's Church Hall, "our garage back home is bigger than this place."

Jonjo gritted his teeth and pointed. "Table tennis over there..."

"One table?"

"Why, how many do you need?" said

Jonjo. He pointed again before Ricky could tell him one for each hand. "Pool table over there, dartboards over there." He emphasised the 's' at the end of dartboards. "Two of them, see."

Ricky nodded slowly as his eyes roamed around the hall. He slipped some gum into his mouth.

"And this is all of it?"

"No." Jonjo pointed towards a door at the far end of the hall. There's a meetings room through there – with armchairs!"

"Wow-eee," sighed Ricky.

As he glared at his new neighbour, Jonjo was suddenly filled with an overwhelming urge to give him an absolute pasting at something, anything, it didn't matter what. Something that would shut him up.

"Want a game of pool?"

Ricky shrugged. "Sure."

The game was over in four minutes flat as Ricky sent balls whizzing into the pockets from all angles.

"Played before, have you?" muttered Jonjo through gritted teeth as they set the balls up again.

"Every day," said Ricky, chewing idly. "We've got a table in our basement back home."

After another four crushing defeats, Jonjo suggested a game of darts instead. "First to five hundred and one, OK?"

"Sure."

Jonjo still had another three hundred and fifty-three to go as Ricky casually flicked in a double twenty to go out.

"Got a board in our basement back home," he shrugged. "Play every day."

Jonjo pointed over to where the table-tennis table had just become free. "Suppose you've got one of those as well, have you?"

Ricky shook his head as he fingered the threadbare net in disgust. "Nope."

"No?" said Jonjo, his hopes rising.

"Not one. Two. One in the basement, one on the back porch..."

By the end of the evening, Jonjo was seething. Having to endure Ricky King's non-stop complaints about how pokey everything was had been no fun. Losing at pool and darts had been worse. But to get annihilated at table tennis with everybody watching – that had been the end. The only thing left to do had been to leave for home as quickly as possible.

"Table tennis your best sport, is it?" asked Ricky as they turned into their road.

Jonjo shook his head. Table tennis was his second-best sport, but he wasn't going to admit that.

"Nah," he said. "I only mess about at table tennis."

"That figures."

"Football is my best sport," said Jonjo through clenched teeth. "I play for The Angels – the youth club's team."

Ricky stopped at his front gate. "The youth club has a football team? I didn't know you played the game over here in England."

Jonjo was just about to explain in no uncertain terms that the game had actually been invented in England when suddenly he realised something. Ricky wasn't talking about the game the Angels played. Americans called that "soccer". He was talking about American Football, with its bulging shoulder pads and crash helmets – the sort Jonjo had seen arriving the day Ricky moved in.

So Ricky was assuming the Angels were an American football team! A very un-angelic thought flicked into Jonjo's mind.

"Yeah, we play. We're not very good, though." He turned to Ricky as though he'd just had the most wonderful idea. "Hey – would you play for us? I bet you're brilliant!"

Ricky looked flattered. "Maybe. I've got all my gear with me."

"You have?" said Jonjo, wide-eyed and innocent.

"Sure. I didn't expect to find a team so fast though."

Jonjo tried to look as enthusiastic as he could. "We haven't got a match tomorrow, so we'll be practising in the park. Ten o'clock. Why don't you come along?"

"OK," said Ricky. "It sounds like you need a player who knows what he's doing. Where do you get changed?"

Jonjo felt a little twinge of conscience. He squashed it quickly.

"Er...they've only got pokey little changing rooms at the park. Why don't you put all your gear on before you come?"

"Right, I will! See you there. Should be fun."

"It certainly should, Ricky baby," muttered Jonjo as he strolled indoors.

2

Soccer, not Socker!

"Who on earth was that kid you brought to the club last night, Jonjo?" asked Lennie Gould, the Angels captain, next morning.

"Ricky King," said Jonjo, juggling a ball on his knee. "He's American. He's just moved in next door to me."

"What a big-head," said Lennie. He trapped the ball as Jonjo flicked it over to him.

"He had something to be big-headed about though, didn't he?" said Kirsten

Browne, the Angels goalkeeper. "Showed you what for, Jonjo."

"Well, I could do without seeing too much of him," said Colin "Colly" Flower, the team's front runner.

"Er...well..." grinned Jonjo. "Actually, I'm hoping we're going to see a fair bit more of him this morning. I've invited him along."

"You'll see," he said as, in the distance, St Jude's Church clock struck ten. "Look…here he comes!"

Ricky had just dashed through the park gate as if he was running out for the start of a match. Charging across to the Angels, he skidded to a halt.

"OK, you guys. Let's show you how this game is played in Dallas…" He stopped, frowning as he saw what Jonjo was wearing. "Say, don't you even get changed into football gear over here?"

"We are changed," sniggered Jonjo.

The others joined in with the fun.

"Come by motorbike, did you?" giggled Lulu Squibb, pointing at the helmet on Ricky's head.

"He's got shoulder pads on as well," hooted Daisy Higgins. "We don't wear pads when we play football, Ricky. Only when we play cricket."

"Then they go on our legs," said Jeremy Emery. "Not under our shirts!"

"We wear shorts as well," said Bazza Watts, looking at Ricky's knee-length breeches, "not longs!"

The American boy suddenly fell in. He swung round to face Jonjo. "You don't play for a football team. You play for a soccer team!"

Ricky looked as if he was about to burst. Snatching off his helmet, he was about to let rip when he caught sight of the Angels coach, Trevor Rowe, coming their way.

Trev had come straight from St Jude's, where he was the vicar. Seeing his cleric's collar made Ricky bite his tongue – at least until Trev said, "Hello. I didn't realise there was an American football team around here."

"There isn't!" exploded Ricky. "Somebody forgot to tell me you call soccer 'football' round here!"

"I didn't?" said Jonjo. "Gee, I'm sorry!"

Trev cooled things down. "You seem to have been the victim of a little joke, Ricky. You're welcome to stay and join in our practice session, though. Have you played football – I mean, soccer – before?"

"Sure," said Ricky. "And – yeah," he added, with a glare at Jonjo, "I'd love to join in."

After some warm-up exercises, Trev sorted everybody out for a seven-a-side game. Just as Ricky had hoped, he was on the opposite side to Jonjo.

As they began to play, though, Ricky was wondering whether he might not have been a bit hasty in wanting to get his revenge. He had played soccer before, he'd told the truth about that. What he hadn't admitted to Trev was that it had only been a couple of times – and that, although he'd learned them once, his knowledge of the rules was very rusty indeed.

Fifteen minutes later, though, he was still waiting for his first touch of the ball.

"Come on!" yelled Trev. "Let's get Ricky into this game!"

In midfield, Lulu Squibb had just won a tackle. As the ball bobbled up she booted it wildly in Ricky's direction, way over the heads of both Bazza Watts and Jonjo Rix on the opposite side.

"Come on, Lulu!" shouted Trev. "How's he supposed to reach that…?" The words died on his lips as Ricky began to run.

Within a few strides, he'd overtaken
Jonjo like a train steaming past a cart-horse.
Ahead of him, Bazza glanced over his
shoulder and saw him coming. Still within
easy reach of the bouncing ball, the Angels
full-back accelerated. It was nowhere near
enough. Within seconds Ricky had gone
past him as though he'd been
standing still.

That's when
it happened. In the
excitement of getting to the ball first,
Ricky's mind did a somersault. Instead of
controlling the bouncing ball with his foot,
he caught it, just as he would have done

during a game of American football! Only after he'd charged over the goal-line and touched the ball down with a whoop of delight did he realise what he'd done.

POF

All over the pitch the Angels players were curled up on the ground, holding their sides as they roared with laughter.

"Handball I think, Ricky," smiled Trev, pointing for the free kick.

His face burning with embarrassment, Ricky trudged slowly back to the half-way line.

"You do know the rules, don't you?" Jonjo hooted at him. "If not, maybe you'd better go in goal!"

Ricky thought hard. Slowly, the rules of soccer came drifting back into his mind – and, as they arrived, one rule in particular shone out among all the others. A rule that gave him a chance of revenge!

That chance came not long afterwards. As Jonjo Rix received a pass from Daisy Higgins, Ricky went to meet him.

"No chance," said Jonjo. With a flick, he pushed the ball past Ricky and sprinted after it. Ricky let him go, then turned and gave chase. In a few quick strides he was level with Jonjo and within reach of the ball...

Wallop!

Hurling himself sideways, Ricky slammed into Jonjo with a mighty shoulder charge, sending Jonjo cartwheeling off the pitch and into a heap of grass cuttings.

"Foul!" yelled every Angels player at once.

Smiling, Trev shook his head. "No foul!" he declared. "A shoulder charge is perfectly legal in football – and soccer!"

It was Ricky's turn to laugh. "Maybe we'd both better check the rules." He held a hand out towards Jonjo. "And I reckon that makes us even. Shake on it, yeah?"

Jonjo peered out from the pile of grass cuttings. His face was twisted in pain. "Forget the rules. Somebody had better check my ankle. I think it's broken!"

3

Red Faces All Round

"No, it's not broken," said Trev after prodding and poking Jonjo's ankle. "You're going to have a bruise, though. It's going to be touch and go whether you'll be fit enough for next Saturday's game against the Wheatley Wasps."

"He's got to be fit!" cried Rhoda O'Neill. "Jonjo always scores against Wasps. Smiler Smith is scared stiff of him!"

"Who?" asked Ricky.

"Smiler Smith," said Rhoda, "Darren Smith, the Wasps' captain. We call him 'Smiler' because he never does – except when he's kicking you up in the air. Jonjo can give him the run-around like nobody else."

"So without him we're struggling," chipped in Tarlock Bhasin.

Trev finished bandaging Jonjo's ankle. "Well, let's see how it goes. Stay away from football for a few days and it could be all right."

Jonjo glared across at Ricky. "I will," he growled. "And American footballers!"

Trev looked from one to the other. "I think it's time you two had a look at your Bibles," he laughed. "Try St Mark's Gospel, chapter twelve, verse thirty."

"Huh?" said Jonjo and Ricky together.

"'Love thy neighbour'!"

Now that, thought Ricky, is not a bad idea. Not a bad idea at all...

It took him some time to persuade his parents and write the invitations out, but by Wednesday he was ready. Ricky hopped over the fence and rang at Jonjo's front doorbell.

"Hi," he said, looking down at Jonjo's bandaged ankle. "How's the injury?"

"Recovering," said Jonjo. "No thanks to you."

"OK, so I got a bit mad. Anyway, it's apology time. Here. Can you come?"

YOU ARE INVITED TO A
HOUSE-WARMING
with a
⭐ :: **HOT DOG!** ⭐
Ricky's place, Friday, 7pm.

"A bit of a party," Ricky went on. "All the Angels are being invited. I've asked a lot of the kids from my class at school to come too."

"Why, having trouble with them as well, are you?" asked Jonjo.

"How'd you guess that?"

"Just a hunch," grinned Jonjo.

"I reckon you'll all get on together anyhow. They play for some soccer team or the other. So, can you come?"

Jonjo looked thoughtful. "Let me check one thing first. Is what you mean by a hot

101

dog the same as what I mean by a hot dog? A long bread roll, the longer the better..."

"Filled with a sausage as thick as your arm," nodded Ricky. "And covered with lashings of tomato sauce?"

"We call it tom-ay-to sauce," said Ricky, pronouncing the word the American way, "but – yeah, you've got it."

"Then I'll be there," said Jonjo.

He never had been able to resist a tasty hot dog. Then again, neither had he ever been able to resist trying to get his own back. And the little idea that had just popped into his head combined the two beautifully!

The delicious smell of sizzling sausages greeted the Angels as they arrived one by one at Ricky's house and were led round to the back garden. Soon they were fighting their way through a massive hot dog as Ricky wielded a huge squeezy tomato-sauce container.

"What do you reckon?" he asked Jonjo.

"OK, you win," said Jonjo. "This is definitely the non-pokiest hot dog I have ever seen!"

"Looks like you've forgiven him, Jonjo," said Daisy Higgins as the front doorbell rang and Ricky handed over his tomato-sauce container before heading back through the house to answer it.

Jonjo nodded slowly. "Not quite," he said, watching Ricky go.

Daisy recognised the look on Jonjo's face. "Why, what are you up to?"

"He gave me a red ankle," said Jonjo. "So it's only fair if I give him something in return, isn't it?"

"Such as?"

Tossing the tomato-sauce container from hand to hand, Jonjo slid into the depths of a laurel bush. "How about a red face?"

He didn't have long to wait. Moments later, he heard the sound of the back door opening and Ricky's voice.

"Hey, everybody. Here's some of the kids from my new school. And guess what? I just found out the name of the soccer team they play for…"

Thrusting the container out from the bush, Jonjo squeezed hard. A jet of tomato sauce shot out with a satisfying whoosh.

"Now we're even!" yelled Jonjo.

He dived out to survey his handiwork, only to discover that the sauce had missed Ricky altogether. The American boy was finishing what he'd started to say.

"They play for the team you're up against tomorrow. Wheatley Wasps! And this," added Ricky, turning to the large, powerful boy standing beside him, "is ..."

"Their captain," snarled the large, powerful boy as he wiped a mighty blob of tomato sauce from his face.

"Darren Smith!" gulped Jonjo.

4

Sting 'em Wasps!

"Why didn't you say you went to the same school as Darren Smith!" yelled Jonjo. "I told you he was Wasps' captain."

"How the heck was I supposed to know he was the same one?" Ricky shouted back. "There's a whole bunch of kids called Smith in our year! Why didn't you say you were going to fire sauce at him?"

"I wasn't. I was firing at you!"

"But you hit me, Jonjo," said Darren Smith. "So now I'm going to hit you. And

it ain't going to be with a blob of sauce.
Is it, Wasps?"

Grouped behind him, the rest of the
Wheatley Wasps team shook their heads
menacingly. Darren Smith took a step
towards Jonjo. Then, noticing his bandaged
ankle, he stopped.

"Hello. How'd you do that, Jonjo? Taking
a corner? Miss the ball and kick the flag? Aah,
poor Jonjo." A smile crossed Darren Smith's
face for the first time since he'd arrived. "I
wanted you on the other side tomorrow."

"I'll be on the other side, don't you
worry," shouted Jonjo. "I'm fit enough
to play."

"Oh, yeah? We'll see about that!"

Jonjo didn't hesitate. As the Wasps' captain darted forward to try and stamp on his ankle, he let him have it with another splurge from the tomato-sauce container he was still holding. Then, as the other Wasps players came racing in he let them have a splurge too.

Then, hurling the sauce container aside, he ran for it.

"Sting him, Wasps!" screamed Darren Smith, turning to give chase as Jonjo shot down the side of the house and out into the street.

Moments later, the Wasps players chased after them – and the rest of the Angels chased off after *them*!

Ricky stood there, stunned. He'd goofed again! Instead of the hot-dog party enabling him and Jonjo to patch things up, any minute now his neighbour was going to experience the complete opposite: Darren Smith was going to take Jonjo apart!

He had to stop Darren. Snatching up the sauce container and racing out into the road, Ricky put his head down and started running.

Ahead of him were the Angels. Within a few strides he'd caught up with the slower runners like Daisy Higgins. Whistling past them, he caught up with the quicker ones, such as Mick Ryall and Rhoda O'Neill. But even they couldn't keep pace with the flying American.

Jetting past them, he quickly found himself amongst the Wasps.

They were strung out across the road, blocking his way. He tried to go round the outside, but they saw him and moved out to stop him. Dodging across, Ricky tried to go

past on the other side. Again, the same thing happened.

"OK, you guys," yelled Ricky. "You asked for it! Make way for a Dallas Cowboy!"

Wallop!

Head down and shoulder forward, as if he was racing for a touchdown, Ricky thundered in between two of the Wasps.

One flew off to the left and collided with a dustbin. The other shot off to the right and somersaulted over a hedge. He was through!

But, up ahead, he could see that Darren Smith had almost caught up with Jonjo. Fast as he was, Ricky wasn't going to get to him in time. There was nothing he could do to prevent Jonjo getting a pasting for covering Darren with tomato sauce.

Unless...

In his hand, Ricky was still holding the container. Could he? It had to be worth a try. Screeching to a halt, he drew

back his arm and launched the sauce bottle into the air...and down...and down...to land slap bang on Darren Smith's head! For Jonjo it was a wonderful moment. As the Wasps' captain was drenched for a third time, everything looked wonderful.

Thanks to his American neighbour he'd been saved from a pounding. What was more, he'd just survived the ultimate fitness test – a half-mile sprint with a crazy Wasp on his heels – and his injured ankle had coped with it brilliantly! There was no doubt about it. He'd definitely be playing in the big match.

"Ricky King," he yelled. "I apologise! I take it all back! You are the greatest!"

And with that, he promptly tripped over the kerb.

"Aagh! My ankle!"

5

Look – No Hands!

Jonjo hobbled into the changing room, his
arm around Ricky's shoulder. He shook his
head hopelessly as Trev looked up.

"It's no use, Trev. I can hardly walk on
it, let alone kick a ball."

"Then we've got problems," said Trev.
"We haven't got a substitute. Lionel
Murgatroyd's dad rang me. Lionel's got
the measles."

"You mean we're down to ten players?"
cried Mick Ryall.

"Afraid so," said Trev. "Unless you've got another suggestion."

"I have." All eyes swung towards Jonjo as he said, "Ricky can take my place."

"Me? You're joking!"

"No, I'm not."

"But I can't play the game," said Ricky. "You saw that the other day."

"Yeah, we know that," said Jonjo. "But the Wasps don't know it, do they? All they know is that you can run like the wind. Just seeing you in an Angels shirt will have their knees knocking!"

"Well…"

"Come on, Trev. What do you reckon?"

The coach nodded slowly. "It's worth a try. Just so long as you remember, Ricky – no picking the ball up!"

⚽   ⚽   ⚽

The Angels and Wheatley Wasps were two evenly matched sides. Both sides managed to do their fair share of attacking, with play swinging from end to end. Out on the wing, Ricky was doing a lot of running up and down without actually touching the ball.

"You're doing fine," said Jonjo to him from the touchline. "Two of them are watching your every move. It's giving Colly more space."

Jonjo was right. With twenty minutes gone, Colly Flower broke through the middle for the Angels. Out on the touchline, the two Wasps defenders shadowing Ricky didn't know which way to turn.

Suddenly, they decided that they had to go for Colly. Racing across, both slid into the tackle at the very moment Colly hit his shot. Ballooning into the air, the ball soared out towards the wing.

Ricky couldn't stop himself. After twenty minutes without touching the ball, he'd once again completely forgotten he was playing soccer. In a flash he'd caught it and was haring down the wing, only to be brought to an embarrassed halt by the shriek of the referee's whistle.

"Deliberate handball. Don't do it again, Number Twelve."

Worse was to come. The free kick was punted into the Angels penalty box where Daisy Higgins and Jeremy Emery, still with half their minds on what had just happened, both left it to each other and allowed Darren Smith to nip in and blast the ball past Kirsten Browne to put Wasps 1-0 ahead.

"Think soccer, Ricky!" yelled Jonjo as the Angels trudged miserably back for the restart. "Not American Football!"

In the centre of the pitch, Darren Smith looked up as he heard Jonjo's cry. Suddenly, he raced back to say something to his own goalkeeper.

The Angels soon found out what he'd said. As their next attack broke down, the Wasps goalkeeper gathered the ball. Instead of hammering it down field towards his own attackers though, he launched his kick in a different direction – high into the air, and straight towards Ricky.

"Ricky!" screamed Jonjo. "Don't…" He wasn't quick enough. Instinctively, Ricky had leapt in the air and caught it. Once again the referee blew for a free kick, but this time he fished in his pocket as well. "Yellow card, Number Twelve. You were warned. One more deliberate handball and I'll be sending you off!"

"That must be Darren Smith's game!" said Rhoda O'Neill to Colly. "They're trying to get Ricky sent off. They're trying to get us down to ten players."

"Then we'll have to keep the ball away from him!" groaned Colly.

He managed it – just. For the final ten minutes of the first half, the Wasps goalie sent every kick he got high in the direction of Ricky, and Colly spent all his time racing across and heading the ball away again.

"I never thought I'd end up having to mark one of my own team," muttered Colly as they trooped off at half-time.

Ricky looked downcast. "Sorry, guys. I just can't get the hang of this game. I reckon you'd be better off playing without me."

Jonjo had hobbled across to join them. "No we wouldn't. If you can only get it through your skull that you can't pick the ball up, you'll cause them all sorts of trouble with your speed."

There was no arguing with that. "Well," said Ricky, "I sure don't have a problem with their full-back. The guy's a tortoise. I could outrun him with one hand tied behind my back."

"With one hand..." Jonjo's eyes lit up. "Hey! How about with both hands tied behind your back?"

"Huh?"

Jonjo turned to Trev. "If we tied both hands behind his back he couldn't handball then, could he?"

Trev looked doubtful. "No, but..."

"There's nothing in the rules to say he can't play with his hands tied is there?"

"No. No, there isn't."

Without another word, Jonjo whipped a lace out of the trainer he couldn't get on his swollen ankle. Then, pulling Ricky's hands together behind his back, he quickly tied them up. "There you go!

You'd have to be a contortionist to commit a handball horror now!"

The second half began. Once more, as an Angels attack was foiled, the Wasps goalie didn't hesitate. With his defenders looking on, he thumped the ball straight out to the unmarked Ricky.

Again, the American boy instinctively went to catch it – only to find that he couldn't move his hands. Instead, the ball plopped against his chest and dropped at his feet.

"Run, Ricky, run!" screamed Jonjo. Too late, the Wasps defence realised what had happened. By then, though, Ricky was hurtling down the wing. Thrown into a panic, three Wasps defenders raced across to try to cut him off, leaving Colly unmarked in the middle. All Ricky had to do was boot it in his general direction. With the freedom of the penalty area, Colly had plenty of time to control the ball before banging it gleefully into the Wasps net for the equaliser.

"Forget the plan!" yelled Darren Smith at once. "Play our normal game!"

From then on, the Wasps slowly gained the upper hand. As they pressed forward with more and more attacks, Ricky saw little of the ball.

"Ricky, switch to the middle!" yelled Colly as, with just a minute to go, Wasps surged onto the attack again. "I'm going back to help the defence!"

The American boy chugged into the centre circle. No sooner had he done so than Colly, seizing on a loose ball in his own penalty area, lashed it as high and as far upfield as he could manage. Ricky was after it in a flash, his arms pumping as he ran.

Arms pumping?

Watching from the touchline, Jonjo looked on in horror. His knot had come undone. Ricky's hands were free! What was more, with his eyes glued to the flying ball high above him, there was no doubt at all in Jonjo's mind that Ricky was preparing to catch it!

"Ricky!" screamed Jonjo. "Don't catch it!!"

But Ricky was already in mid-jump, timing his leap to perfection. His hands were above his head, ready to catch the ball.

Hearing Jonjo's shout, there was only one thing he could do. Flinging his arms wide apart, he let the ball thud down onto the top of his head.

"Aww!" groaned Ricky.

As the ball bounced away, he collapsed in a heap, his head feeling as if it was being pounded from the inside by dozens of tiny boxing gloves.

To make matters worse, moments later Colly and the other Angels raced up, dragged him to his feet and began to shout and hoot in his ear!

"What a header!" yelled Colly.

"Brilliant!" shouted Lulu Squibb.

"Their goalie didn't see it!" hooted Rhoda O'Neill.

Dumbly, his head still ringing like a bell, Ricky focused on the Wheatley Wasps goal. Something was nestling in the back of the net. Something round and soccer-ball shaped...

"What..." he stammered.

"Ricky, man!" yelled Jonjo, hopping up and down in spite of his injured ankle, "you scored!"

❀   ❀   ❀

"A two-one victory, Jonjo," said Tarlock Bhasin as they trooped happily back into the changing room, "and you know what they say..."

"Never change a winning team," said Jeremy Emery. "You could have a job getting your place back, Jonjo. Ricky the Rocket may take some shifting."

"No, he won't," droned Ricky, still a bit stunned. "I'm retiring from soccer as of today."

Trev laughed as he sloshed some cold water on the back of his neck. "Don't be too hasty, Ricky. Come along for a few training sessions."

"Yeah," said Jonjo. "Give us time to teach you the rules!"

Ricky grinned. "Well…OK. I'll come along. On one condition."

"What's that?"

Ricky winced as he felt the bump on his head. "You let me wear my helmet!"

MIDFIELD MADNESS

CONTENTS

1

Operation Lulu!

Tuesday was training night for the Angels
FC team. Officially, it was an opportunity to
try out tactics and have an enjoyable
kick-about, but nobody could have guessed
this from the way Lulu Squibb was playing.
As far as she was concerned, there was no
such thing as training. She tried just as hard,
and got just as wound up, as if she was
playing in a real match!

Whirling into a tackle, Lulu whipped the
ball from the toes of Lionel Murgatroyd, the

Angels' regular substitute, and raced off down the pitch. Tricking her way past Mick Ryall with a nifty body swerve, she closed in on goal.

Another couple of steps, she thought, and then...

"Ooomph!"

Just as Lulu was preparing to let fly with a shot hard enough to break the net, Daisy Higgins looped one of her long legs round from behind and tripped her up.

"Daisy rotten Higgins!" screamed Lulu, leaping to her feet. "I'll knock your block off!"

Only the fierce shriek of a whistle stopped Lulu carrying out her threat.

"Calm down, Lulu, calm down!" cried the team's coach, Trevor Rowe, who was refereeing the practice game as usual. Placing the ball at Lulu's feet, he murmured, "Concentrate. Come on, they're not looking. You can hit them with a quick free kick."

"Good thinking, Trev," said Lulu, seeing just what he meant. Most of the Angels defenders were looking the other way.

She glanced to her left. Colin 'Colly' Flower was in the clear. If she whipped it out to him quickly he'd have a clear run on goal.

She drew her foot back...only to see the ball disappear as Jeremy Emery ran past and flicked it away.

Lulu's eyes flashed. "You big prune! He kicked the ball away. Book him for time-wasting, Trev!"

"Lulu, it's not a proper match."

"Book him for having dirty knees, then!
Book him for having a tongue-twister
name like Jeremy Emery! I don't care,
just book him!"

Trev wagged a gentle finger in the
centre-back's direction. "Fair play, Jeremy.
Remember the Angels code: 'Angels on and
off the pitch'!"

"He'll remember it if I get my hands on
him!" yelled Lulu, going red in the face. "I'll
turn him into a real angel!"

Colly Flower hurried over to replace the ball. "Get ready, Lulu. I'll lay it off for you. You can take a shot."

Still seething, Lulu stepped back five or six paces to give herself a good run in. Trev's whistle blew. Just as he'd promised, Colly slid the ball invitingly to the side. But just as Lulu was going to surge forward and smack it with all her might, the large shape of Jonjo Rix stepped squarely in front of her.

"Get out of my way, you great lummock!" she yelled.

Jonjo showed no sign of doing what he was told. In fact, as Lulu moved to her right to try to get round him, Jonjo moved to the right as well. She skipped to her left. Immediately, Jonjo went that way too, still blocking her path.

With a snarl of rage, Lulu tried the only thing she could think of. Dropping to her knees, she tried scrambling between Jonjo's legs.

But, as she got halfway through, Jonjo snapped his legs together like a vice. She couldn't move forward – and she couldn't move back either!

"Let me go, you big elephant! Foul, Trev! Obstruction! Red card!"

Even as she was yelling, though, Lulu was looping her hands around Jonjo's ankles. With a furious tug, she yanked them forward.

"Aaaarrggh!" cried the hefty Angels striker in surprise, as his feet lifted off the ground and he found himself toppling over.

Almost before he hit the ground, Lulu had leapt free and was jumping on top of him.

"You great lump! I'll teach you to get in my way! I'll put your lights out!"

"Peace!" giggled Jonjo, unable to keep a straight face.

Trev gave a long, loud blast on his whistle. "Full time! End of Operation Lulu!"

Eleven pairs off hands lifted Lulu into the air and began to carry her back to the changing rooms.

Operation Lulu? It had been a set-up!

❀   ❀   ❀

"Well everybody," said Trev once they were all seated. "Operation Lulu seemed to work spectacularly well."

Lulu looked up. All the Angels players were grinning broadly. "Operation Lulu?" she asked. "What do you mean?"

141

"Trev told us to annoy you deliberately," said Lennie Gould, the team's captain.

Lulu glared at Trev. "Why? You know I get annoyed if I'm annoyed!"

"And so do the team we're playing on Saturday – Ashley Wanderers," said Trev.

"The team your cousin Roysten plays in goal for, remember?" added Tarlock Bhasin.

"Of course I remember," said Lulu. "That's why I always play well against them. There's nothing I like better than banging a couple of goals past Roysten."

"And it's because you always play well against them that they try to get you to lose your temper," said Daisy Higgins. "Remember last time?"

Lulu nodded. "Roysten wiped his filthy goalkeeper's glove on my shirt, so I gave him a mouthful – of mud." She hooted with laughter. "He nearly swallowed it!"

Trev was serious, though. "But what also happened was that the referee booked you, and I had to bring you off before you were sent off. That's why we held Operation Lulu tonight – to give you some practice at not losing your temper!"

"And, er...how did I do?"asked Lulu, quietly.

"Terrible!" they all shouted.

Lulu gave an embarrassed smile. "Really? Crumbs. And you didn't even do the thing that annoys me most of all!"

"What's that?" called Bazza Watts. "I'll try it next practice night!"

"I'm not saying," replied Lulu. She gave Bazza a glare. "But you'd know if you did it. I'd go into orbit – and so would you!"

Trev cut the debate short. "Well, if you don't want me bringing you off again this Saturday, Lulu, you'd better hope you've used up your midfield madness for the week."

"I won't let you down, Trev," Lulu told the coach a few minutes later, after she'd got changed and was on her way out.

Trev smiled. "Think beautiful thoughts. That's what I do."

"Think beautiful thoughts," echoed Lulu. "Right." She opened the door, then groaned. "Oh, yes. I'll be going straight to Ashley's ground on Saturday, Trev.

And you'll never guess – I'll be with Roysten. Mum and Dad have gone away for a few days and they've arranged for me to stay with him and Uncle Hubert."

"With Roysten?" called Lennie Gould as he overheard. "Well, just make sure he doesn't find out what really makes you lose your temper, or you can bet he'll try it during the game."

"Don't worry, he won't find out," said Lulu. "That's my secret – and it's staying that way!

145

Pushing through the door, she went outside – only to bump straight into her cousin Roysten. He was leaning against the changing-room wall.

"I've come to meet you," he said miserably.

"Oh, how kind," said Lulu. "Or did Uncle Hubert make you?"

"He made me, of course," growled Roysten. His face suddenly broke into a smile. "But now I'm glad he did."

A nasty feeling hit Lulu. "Why?" she asked. He pointed to the open changing-room window above his head. "Because if I hadn't, I wouldn't have heard you talking about your secret, would I? And now I've got until Saturday to find out what it is!"

2

Think Beautiful Thoughts

Roysten lived on the outskirts of town, in a large, rambling and extremely old house. It was so old, it was said to have at least one hidden tunnel. Lulu could well believe it. If the tunnel began somewhere in the garden it would be the best-hidden tunnel in the world because, apart from a large mown square of grass in the centre, the rest of the garden resembled a jungle.

"Gardening? Bah!" Uncle Hubert would say. "Complete waste of time. I've got much

147

more important things to do!"

Exactly what the important things were that Uncle Hubert spent his time on, Lulu wasn't too sure. He was a scientist of some sort, and had his own laboratory in the basement of the house. Lulu had never seen inside it. The closest she'd ever got was when she had wandered down into the basement on one of her visits and had seen the solid wooden door with its large "Danger! No Entry! Keep Out!" signs.

Just in case she was in any doubt Uncle Hubert mentioned it the moment they sat down for supper.

"It's lovely to have you here to stay, Lulu," he said, cheerfully. "Make yourself at home. Regard the house as your own. Go anywhere you like…" – then his bushy eyebrows dipped and he fixed Lulu with his wild professor's look – "…except into the basement. Do not, repeat, NOT, go down into the basement. I am on the verge of a great discovery, one I've been hunting for for years and years – and I do not want my equipment wrecked by a whistling football!"

Roysten was sitting on the other side of the table. "I don't suppose Lulu will want to play football," he sneered. "She won't want to give away any of her secrets."

"Ah, yes," said Uncle Hubert to Lulu. "Roysten told me your team are playing his on Saturday."

"That's right, Uncle Hubert. Though one thing's no secret. The fact that Angels are going to give Ashley the biggest whacking—owwww!"

Lulu gave a sudden yelp as Roysten suddenly gave *her* a sharp kick on the ankle under the cover of the table.

"Anything wrong, my dear?" asked Uncle Hubert.

Lulu was about to tell him exactly what was wrong when, just in time, Trev's words came floating into her mind. Think beautiful thoughts! It worked. Instead of yelling, Lulu contented herself with thinking the beautiful thought of thumping the ball straight into Roysten's ugly mug during their coming match.

"Nothing wrong at all, Uncle Hubert," she said, sweetly – but made sure she kept her ankles well out of the way for the rest of supper.

Keeping completely out of Roysten's way over the next few days was a lot harder, though. His tactic was to pop up when she least expected him and try something to see if it made her lose her temper.

He suddenly appeared behind her when she was at the top of the stairs next morning.

"Does an elbow in the ribs do it, I wonder?" he scowled, before giving her one.

Sent off balance, Lulu would have fallen headlong down the stairs if she hadn't leapt onto the bannisters and slid down instead.

"Watch it, you!" snapped Lulu. Then Trev's advice came into mind again, making her think of Roysten sitting in a puddle as she dribbled rings round him. "I mean, silly me! Bashing your elbow with my ribs like that. Is it all right?"

On Thursday morning Lulu tried to stay out of Roysten's way by not getting up at all, but pretending to be asleep. It didn't work. As she was lying in bed the door creaked open and a feather on a stick came stretching through and began to tickle the soles of her feet.

"Gerroutofit!!" she yelled.

"Is that your secret thing you hate, I wonder?" called Roysten.

"You'll find out if I get hold of you!" Leaping out of bed, Lulu chased after her cousin – only to be tripped up by the length of string he'd stretched across the doorway.

"Aaarrggh!"

Landing nose first, Lulu hurtled across the polished floor as if she'd been fouled by an expert. She leapt up, her fists clenched.

"Come 'ere, Roysten! I'm going to…" – but once again Trev's words came into mind – "…score against you on Saturday," she trilled, sweetly. "You see if I don't."

Now it was Roysten's turn to get mad.

"All right. I've tried the gentle things. I've tried ankle-tapping. I've tried nudging you in the ribs. I've tried tickling and I've tried tripping. So if none of those are your secret, then I can see it's time I turned nasty!"

Lulu sighed as Roysten stormed off downstairs. Trev's advice had really helped, and she had done well. Sooner or later, though, Roysten was going to do the thing that really sent her wild. It was so obvious, she couldn't understand why he hadn't tried it yet.

So how could she stay out of his way for the rest of the day? The idea came to her as she looked out of the window and saw the mown patch of grass in the middle of Uncle Hubert's jungle garden.

Lulu strolled to the top of the stairs. "Hey, Roysten! How about a kick-about in the garden? Three goals and in."

3

A Bold Experiment

Lulu set up a goal just in front of the most overgrown part of the garden.

"You want to go in goal first, Roysten?" she asked.

Roysten agreed. "OK. Maybe your secret is that you get really mad when your best shots are saved by a brilliant keeper!"

To start with, Lulu hit a couple of gentle shots that even Uncle Hubert could have saved. Then she tried six in a row that were all deliberately wide, so that Roysten had to

157

scramble amongst the overgrown bushes
behind their goal to get the ball back. It was
immediately after his sixth
retrieval, as he stood in
goal puffing and
panting, that Lulu put
her plan into action.

Taking careful aim,
she hammered the ball
high over Roysten's
head and into the
deepest part of the
undergrowth.

Her cousin groaned.
"You can get that one."

Lulu cheerfully plunged into the jungle.
Deeper and deeper she went, reaching parts
that looked as though they hadn't been
touched in centuries. She found the ball, not
far away from the tall tree at which she'd
aimed. And then...she went even further

into the undergrowth. She found the bushiest bush ever – and sat down.

Perfect! What a plan! All she had to do was hide here for the rest of the day and Roysten couldn't annoy her or try any other trick to discover her secret.

She didn't answer when Roysten, sounding far away, called, "Lulu! Haven't you found it yet?" Soon, she hoped, he would give up waiting and go away.

That was the flaw in her plan. Roysten didn't go away. She'd only been in her hiding place for a few minutes when she heard him crunching through the undergrowth towards her. "I've just worked out what you're up to. You're hiding from me. Well it won't work!"

Lulu decided it was time to move. Crawling on all fours, she pushed her way further into the jungle.

Cra-ack!

At the sound of splintering wood, Lulu felt something give way beneath her hand. Looking down she saw a rotten wooden trapdoor – and, beneath it, there was a gaping hole...

"It's one of the hidden tunnels," gasped Lulu. "It must be!"

She pulled away the rest of the mouldy trapdoor and hopped down. It *was* a tunnel! She could see a square of light at the far end.

Perhaps it led back into the house? If it did, Roysten would never find her!

Lulu crept towards the light – and discovered why it was square-shaped. It was oozing out from the four sides of a small door, with a rusty iron handle. Lulu held her breath and pushed. The door squeaked open to reveal…a room full of benches and cupboards, test-tubes and bubbling glass containers. She'd come out through a fake panel in the wall of Uncle Hubert's laboratory!

There was no sign of Uncle Hubert. Perhaps she could just take a little look around? Throwing her pigtails over her shoulder, Lulu crept through the gap and into the brightly lit laboratory...

"Gotcha!"

As she felt her pigtails given a mighty tug from behind, Lulu jumped wildly into the air. She shook her head like a maniac. It was no good. Roysten, who had found the passage and followed her down, still had her pigtails tightly in his hands. He tugged again. The effect was dramatic.

"Let go!" screamed Lulu. "I'll mangle you! I'll pulverise you! I'll tear you limb from limb if you don't LET GO OF MY HAIR!"

Behind her, Roysten whooped in triumph. "That's your secret! I bet it is! You can't stand having your pigtails pulled!" He gave them another hard tug, to test his theory.

Lulu shot backwards. Whirling round to give him a thump, she accidentally knocked a bubbling jar of green liquid off Uncle Hubert's work-bench and onto the floor. Other equipment clattered over. Lulu spun again.

163

This time she managed to wrench herself free, but as she did so, she thumped against the bench, causing a huge test-tube full of red gunge to smash on the floor and mix with the green stuff.

"It *is* your secret!" crowed Roysten, delightedly.

"All right, now you know!" cried Lulu. Her cousin was edging nearer, his hands outstretched.

Lulu backed away – into the red and green mixture on the floor. Suddenly, it felt as if the soles of her trainers were made of ice, only a thousand times more slippery. Shooting off backwards, she slithered into a tall cupboard. Down it came with a crash.

"Oh, no!" groaned Lulu.

Her secret discovered, the laboratory wrecked. What else could go wrong?

Only one thing. At that very moment, the laboratory door opened and in stepped Uncle Hubert.

4

Eureka!

"What have you done!" bellowed Uncle Hubert, bristling with rage.

"I found a tunnel," wailed Lulu. "I didn't know it led into here. Then Roysten came up behind me and pulled my—"

"Roysten?" growled Uncle Hubert, looking around. "Roysten isn't here."

He was right. Roysten wasn't there. While her eyes had been on Uncle Hubert's arrival, Roysten must have dived back into the tunnel and shut the fake door behind him. She

166

couldn't even see where it was!

"Well, he was," Lulu stormed, the words tumbling out. "He pulled my hair so I swung round to sock him one but I missed and hit one of your jars instead so I had another swing but I missed again and hit a test-tube and then I saw him coming for me so I tried to get away and I slipped and knocked the cupboard over and...and..." She looked at Uncle Hubert's furious face. "...You're not happy, are you?"

"No, I am not happy!" yelled Uncle Hubert. "And if I'm not happy, then I'm going to make quite sure that you're not happy either."

"H-how?"

"By making you clear this mess up on Saturday instead of playing football!"

⚽   ⚽   ⚽

Lulu picked up the laboratory telephone and dialled Trev's number.

"No need for great explanations," said Uncle Hubert, almost breathing down her neck. "Just tell him that you can't play in the match."

Lulu's mind was in a whirl. She'd tried her hardest to get Uncle Hubert to change his mind. "I can't let them down. They'll be expecting me to turn up."

"Then you can telephone and say you won't be there!" had been his stern reply.

So that's what she was doing – calling Trev to give him the bad news. As the phone rang at the other end, Lulu thought frantically. She simply *had* to play on Saturday. Somehow she'd have to get Uncle Hubert to change his mind between now and the game. So, what she definitely didn't want to do now was tell Trev that she couldn't play. He'd go straight off and give her place to their usual substitute, Lionel Murgatroyd. But telling Trev she couldn't play on Saturday was exactly what Uncle Hubert *did* want her to say! What on earth could she do?

At the other end the ringing stopped. There was a short pause and then an electronic voice said, "This is St Jude's Church. I'm sorry, but Trevor Rowe isn't here at the moment. Please leave your message after the beep."

Lulu's eyes lit up. "It's an answering machine!" She went to put the phone down. "I'd better leave it, eh?"

"Leave it?" snapped Uncle Hubert. "Quite right. You will leave your message."

Lulu sighed. There was no way out. "Hello, Trev," she said. "It's Lulu. I just rang to say that I can't play…"

That was when she had her brainwave. As a whirring sound came from the other end of the line she added, "in goal on Saturday!"

She clicked the phone down with hope in her heart. It was a perfect solution. All it needed was for Trev to realise that, as Lulu never had played in goal, a message from her saying that she *couldn't* play in goal meant that she *could* play in any other position!

On Saturday morning, Roysten set off for the game with a smug look on his face.

"Look on the bright side," he sneered, "if you were playing you wouldn't stay on the pitch for long. Now I know your secret, I'd get you sent off in the first minute!"

Feeling dismal, Lulu went down to the basement. She'd thought and thought about how she might escape from Uncle Hubert but still hadn't come up with an idea. But then, as she entered the laboratory, she saw a way.

Uncle Hubert was already there. He'd cleaned up the broken glass and was unloading new test-tubes and jars from a very tall walk-in cupboard. What's more, it was a cupboard with a lock – and he'd left the key in it! That had to be the solution. She would lock him in, go off to play in the match – and then worry about what would happen to her afterwards.

Lulu waited until Uncle Hubert went into the cupboard again. Then, creeping round by the bench so that he couldn't see her, Lulu got nearer and nearer until…she slipped once again in the patch of red and green gunge that was in a puddle on the floor!

"Waaaahhhh!"

Once again it felt as though she was skating on incredibly slippery ice. Struggling to stay upright, she shot across the room and straight into Uncle Hubert as he came out of the cupboard.

"Ooooompph!"

"It's that stuff!" cried Lulu as they untangled themselves. "That's what made me slip before!"

Bending to inspect the puddle, Uncle Hubert dabbed at it with his finger. He pulled out a pair of tweezers and tested the edges.

Then, to Lulu's surprise – and to Uncle Hubert's joy – he peeled it up from the floor in one large jelly-like piece. "Amazing! Wonderful!" cried Uncle Hubert. "I've been searching for this for years!" He took Lulu in his arms and waltzed her round the laboratory a couple of times, before asking her anxiously, "How did you manage it? Try to remember, Lulu, it's vitally important!"

Lulu knew exactly how she'd done it. "It was the jar of bubbling green stuff which got mixed up with the test-tube of red gunge. But – why? You mean you actually *want* to make slippery blobs like that?"

"Oh, yes!" cried Uncle Hubert. "Look at it!" He dropped the blob back onto the floor. "It's as slippery as ice on top, and although it sticks firmly to the floor, it can be peeled off easily."

"But what use is it?"

"It means no more bad backs for people who want to lift heavy things, that's what! You just spread this mixture on the floor, slide the heavy object across it to where you want it, then peel the blob up and save it for the next time you need it. Brilliant!"

Humming delightedly, Uncle Hubert filled dozens of test-tubes with green liquid and red gunge. "Wonderful! Marvellous!" he said to himself. Then, looking at Lulu looking at him, a big beam crossed his face.

"Are you still here? I thought you had a football match!"

Lulu's eyes lit up. "You mean...? Yes, I have!"

She darted for the door – then stopped. Uncle Hubert's back was turned. It would only take a moment, and it could be the answer to her other problem...

Moments later she was on her way.

Behind her, Uncle Hubert was so excited about his new discovery that he didn't even notice that one of his test-tubes full of slippery stuff had disappeared.

5

Tug-of-War!

Lulu reached the ground with five minutes to spare. As she raced across to the changing rooms she saw that most of the Angels players were already out on the pitch.

She met a surprised Trev at the changing-room door. "But – the message on my answering machine…you said you couldn't play!"

"I said I couldn't play *in goal*," said Lulu. "I was in a spot of bother. You were supposed to work out that it meant I *could*

178

play in my usual position."

"No," said Trev firmly. "The message definitely said, 'I can't play.' That's all. I remember because it was right at the end of the tape."

"The whirring noise," cried an agonised Lulu, recalling the sound she'd heard while she was on the phone. "That must have been your tape running out. You didn't get the last part of my message!"

The Angels coach sighed. "I'm sorry, Lulu. When I thought you couldn't play I told Lionel Murgatroyd he'd be taking your place.

He's out on the pitch now. You'll have to be substitute, Lulu. I'll put you on in the second half."

Lionel, as an Angels substitute, hardly ever got to start a game. Lulu was pleased for him, but – no, not in her place!

"Sub?" yelled Lulu. "Sub! I can run rings around Ashley Wanderers, you said so yourself."

"Only if you can keep your temper."

"I can," said Lulu, desperately. "I know I can."

"I don't reckon so," came a voice from the door. It was Roysten, changed and on his way out to the pitch, his massive goalkeeping gloves under his arm. "Because I know your little secret, don't I, Lulu? And so do the rest of my team now!"

As Roysten trotted off laughing, Trev shook his head. "That's it, then. Sorry, Lulu. Substitute you'll have to be – and I'm not even sure I'll be able to risk bringing you on at all."

The match began with Lulu fuming on the touchline.

It quickly became obvious that the team were missing her in midfield. Lionel Murgatroyd was enthusiastic, but not much else. He seemed to spend most of his time chasing the ball rather than winning it. Ashley repeatedly launched attacks through the middle of the field that Lulu's tigerish tackling would have stopped.

Then, when the Angels did manage to get forward themselves, they found Roysten playing brilliantly in the Ashley goal with every cross and shot seeming to land slap-bang in the middle of his huge gloves.

"Will I get on in the second half?" Lulu asked at half-time, with the Angels lucky that the score was still 0–0.

"Maybe," said Trev. "Let's see how it goes." It didn't go well.

As another Angels cross was plucked out of the air by Roysten, Lulu's cousin threw the ball quickly into midfield with Lionel Murgatroyd stranded miles out of position.

Surging forward in numbers, the Ashley players combined well. A quick one-two, a measured through-ball, and within moments their striker was banging the ball past Kirsten Browne and into the Angels net.

1–0 to Ashley!

On the touchline, Lulu pleaded, "Trev, put me on!"

Trev looked undecided. "I don't know, Lulu. If you lose your temper…"

I WILL NOT LOSE MY TEMPER!

"Er…let's leave it a little longer, eh?" Trev left it a little longer… and a little longer… until, with just over five minutes to go and Angels no closer to scoring the equaliser, he finally said, "OK, Lulu. Get ready. You're going on."

"Brilliant! I'll just warm up."

But instead of haring up and down the touchline, as substitutes normally do before they come on, Lulu raced only as far as the sports bag she'd brought out with her from the changing room. She knelt there for a few moments, then leapt to her feet.

"Ready, Trev. Let me at 'em!"

As the Angels winger, Mick Ryall, won a corner on the right, the referee waved Lulu on. She raced immediately into the heart of the Ashley penalty area. Roysten saw her coming.

"Well, well," he said, as Lulu planted herself right under his nose on the goal-line. "Look who it isn't. Pigtail Patsy. Maybe I'll just give 'em a little tweak."

"Don't even think about it, Roysten," growled Lulu.

"Whadda-madda-den? Will it make baby scream and shout, will it?"

"Pull my pigtails and you'll see what it does," snarled Lulu, not moving away.

"Pull 'em?" said Roysten. "Thanks for the invitation. I think I will."

Leaning forward, he wrapped one huge goalkeeper's glove around each pigtail and pulled hard.

An instant later, Roysten found himself holding nothing but thin air.

"You'll have to do better than that," laughed Lulu.

Roysten tried again. But again the same thing happened. He wrapped a glove round each pigtail, pulled – and once again found them slithering out of his grasp.

"What have you put on them?" he squawked.

"Ask Uncle Hubert," laughed Lulu. "It's his new wonder invention. I smothered my pigtails with a test-tube full just before I came on!"

Laughing in triumph, she ran back to her usual spot whenever the Angels took a corner – on the edge of the penalty area. Out on the right, Mick Ryall swung the kick across. Normally he was very accurate, but this time he put it too close to the Ashley goal.

"Keeper's!" bellowed Roysten.

As she saw him leap towards the ball, a sudden thought struck Lulu. She'd put Uncle Hubert's slippery stuff on her pigtails, and Roysten had tried to grab those same pigtails... Maybe Roysten's gloves...?

She raced back into the penalty area, arriving just as the ball thumped into Roysten's gloves – and slithered out again! As it dropped at her feet, Lulu simply had to tap it into the net for the equaliser! Angels 1 – Ashley 1!

The game restarted. Immediately, Lulu whirled into a ruck of Ashley players to try to win the ball back.

"Grab them pigtails!" yelled somebody. "It drives her wild!"

Hands reached out, but all slid off harmlessly. Lulu, able to concentrate on what she was doing, won the ball with a crunching tackle. Breaking free, she looked up. In the Ashley goal a mystified Roysten, still trying to work out what had happened, was inspecting his gloves. He wasn't even aware that they'd kicked off again.

Without a second thought, Lulu thumped the ball towards the Ashley goal.

"Roysten!"

The shouts from his team-mates caused Roysten to look up. Lulu groaned. She hadn't hit her shot terribly well and her cousin would now have plenty of time to gather it.

As the ball bounced up to him, Roysten held out his hands to catch it. No sooner had it landed in his gloves, though, than it squirted out again. He tried to pick it up again, but once more it shot out of his gloves – this time over his shoulder.

Roysten turned. The ball was trickling towards his goal. In a panic he dived onto it.